An Italian Sisterhood
A memoir of 3 sisters
by **Olga Cossi**

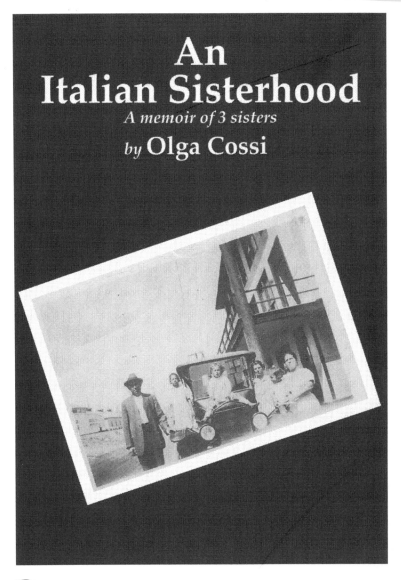

Dear Joelen & Thomby —
How can I say how much you
mean to me — and Don?
Love, Olga Cossi

An Italian Sisterhood

Olga Cossi

Editor in Chief – Nik Morton

Publisher's Note:

Cover and interior: photos courtesy of the author

This is a work of nonfiction.

Solstice Publishing - www.solsticepublishing.com

Revised June 2012 (NM)

Dedication

To my two sisters, and to sisterhood everywhere.

Chapter One

We Were Dudes

Mama tried to get me at a very early age to acknowledge my old-world ties and admit that I was an Italian. My first reaction was to rebel. Even though I was a very little girl, I made my own Declaration of Independence: "I'm an American!" My mother reminded me of that occasionally, claiming those were my first words. But time has a way of mellowing our convictions. Years later I have come to realize what strong and resilient connections we have with our ethnic roots. At last, I am ready to admit that those very roots I refused to acknowledge were the force behind the independence I claimed.

What was there about being an American rather than an Italian that attracted me? Like many children, I came to the conclusion that because my parents were foreign-born, somehow that made me a second class citizen. I associated being Italian with being inferior, even though I knew our parents loved us and thought we were special. When I was old enough to go to a movie theater, I noticed that the underworld characters were often Italian. They spoke broken English. They came from poor neighborhoods. Somehow, those negative images were more impressive than all the wonderful accomplishments in science, music, and the arts for which Italy is famous. Not until I was grown up did I learn that each country and culture has made unique contributions to human advancement. Because I didn't know that, I stubbornly refused to relate to anything that wasn't American.

My most persistent and powerful relationship was with my sister, Rina, almost three years my senior. She was more than my sister. She was my confidant. She was my all, period. She gave me the courage to believe in myself. Of course I loved my parents, but when you are a young child, your parents are like a pair of parentheses that try to hold you in. I looked to Rina for the freedom to be myself, even though I had no idea what that really meant. Still, when I think of my childhood, I think of her.

I have waited a long time to tell this story of our Italian sisterhood. First, I had to learn that having a foreign ethnic background is not something to be ashamed of. For most of us, it is what being an American is all about. Individually and together, my parents like in most cases influenced me more than I was willing to admit. I grew up without ethnic prejudice. Two of our closest family friends were named Brown and Schwartz. I heard say they were Jewish, but I thought that meant sort of like being Sicilian, coming from another part of Italy. I loved them. We were as at home in their house as they were in ours.

On the whole, it was Mama rather than Papa who tried to discipline us and teach us to distinguish between doing right and doing wrong. As a young child, I didn't have a clue that until you learn that, you are in a jam. I was so independent I couldn't stand to be told what to do and what not to do. Going through life without learning that basic lesson is like trying to go the wrong way on a freeway. To get anywhere, you have to be headed in the right direction. You follow the road even though you did not pave it yourself. The traffic rules are there to help you make headway, not to keep you from getting ahead. I refused to learn that. So instead of letting my mother teach me a few important facts, I trusted in Rina.

It was unfair of me to put my sister on the spot of being my "everything". Partly because she was sickly as a child, both Mama and Papa spoiled her. They were afraid for her. I don't remember one time when she was reprimanded. She said and did what she wanted and got away with it. As her little sister, I soon learned the lesson that *who* you were mattered, not what you did. Rina let nothing cloud the aura of confidence she basked in. Her self-confidence was absolute and unchallenged. In her eyes, and in mine, she was Caterina the Great. She was royalty. I was a mouse. I was happy to nibble on the crumbs that fell from her throne.

We had an older sister, Anne, who was an alien as far as Rina and I were concerned. We loved her dearly, but she was not like us. In a word, she was good. Even when we tried hard, we were never really good. So, in our minds, she was a dud. We were dudes. She had no imagination. She was content to do things like clean house and play the piano. She was guilty of what was to us the worse possible

8

sin: she was boring. Bonding with her was out of the question.

Of course, Rina and I eventually gained a different perspective. Both of us became good house keepers and both of us would have loved to be able to play the piano like Anne, but it took years of growing up to get to that point. When we were kids, growing up was the last thing on our minds. I don't think we had much more on our minds than having fun and exploring life. We followed the typical pattern of getting as much out of each day as we could possibly manage regardless of how we did it. Being good like Anne seemed out of our reach, so why try? We contented ourselves with being fun-loving brats. The mischief Rina didn't think of, I did. Together, there wasn't much we wouldn't try.

My relationship with Rina deepened during our annual vacations in Santa Cruz, California, which continued until I was eighteen. Papa and Mama followed the European tradition of taking time off from work to enjoy the beach in the summer. If they had financial worries, I never heard about them. I didn't think in terms of money. I knew that both Mama and Papa came from poor families but their gratitude for what America provided them far outweighed what they endured to get here. They had talked to us about Mussolini and apparently liked some of the things he did for Italy although not his methods of achieving them. To us, all that was in the past. We had today to think about.

Papa especially never looked back. He was an American. Here he could work hard and make a good living. He was content to be able to afford to take his family on vacation each year, and as far as I was concerned that was all that mattered. It was a wonderful way of life and very Italian, although I did not know it at the time. I didn't realize that taking the time to smell the flowers was part of the old-world heritage I wanted nothing to do with.

So year after year, as soon as school was out Mama and Papa bundled us into the car and drove to the beach resort town of Santa Cruz. This was not just a weekend getaway. They rented a cabin close to the Boardwalk where we stayed all summer. My sisters tell me that sometimes Papa had to go back home for a few days, but I don't remember that. Rina and I were having too much fun for me to miss him or anyone.

I was only an infant when these vacations started. My parents had to harness me to a stake to keep me out of the water. Papa loved the beach as much as we did, although Mama never went near the water and never learned to swim. He used to light up his pipe and puff away as he floated on his back just beyond the breakers. My sisters have no recollection of this, but I can see him clearly in my mind's eye, totally content and relaxed. How I envied him!

Rina and I had a love/hate relationship with the ocean. We were more interested in building sand castles and beach combing than in swimming. Both of us enjoy swimming only when our feet were in contact with a firm foundation that made us feel secure. We loved the sandy beach but the fear of being overcome by the waves never left us. I'm not sure why Rina was so afraid of the ocean, but I know why I was.

Years before when we were picnicking on the river near our home, Papa decided to teach me to swim. He took me in his arms and swam out into the deep channel. I was as happy as a lark, secure in his embrace. Then, just like that, he let go of me and told me to swim. I sank like a rock. Instead of lifting me up for air, he stayed just beyond my reach trying to encourage me to swim. By the time he realized that his sink-or-swim method wasn't going to work with me, my lungs were bursting. Even more devastating, my mind was overwhelmed by the fear of water which I have never been able to outgrow completely.

That same fear of water probably protected us, however, when Rina and I took off to explore the beaches in Santa Cruz, alone and early in the morning. We would head out with no regard for the tide. If we got trapped by the incoming surge of the sea, we would climb up on the rocks and wait for the waves to recede. We felt as free literally as the ocean breeze. It was a wonderful, daring time in our lives, and we really lived it up.

When I say, "lived it up", I'm using an Italian yardstick. Although we didn't know it, the cabin we rented was in the "barrio" district of the resort community. It was as close to the beach as we could get, which is all that mattered to us. At night, we had the Boardwalk to enjoy. Once a day we got to pick a ride, usually the merry-go-round because that's what Rina liked, and once in a while we got a treat, cotton candy, a hot dog, or a caramel apple. It sounds like so little to me now.

I can imagine what a young teenager of today would think about spending a whole day at the Santa Cruz Boardwalk and going on only one ride. Fortunately, we didn't know we were not rich. The idea never entered our heads. We had so much, Mama and Papa, each other, a sea full of shells, and miles and miles of white sandy beach.

The Boardwalk has a stage built right on the sand where people can sit and enjoy watching the free shows that are still popular. In those days, if I recall correctly, there were performances at least several times a week if not nightly. We didn't miss a one. Our favorites were the "amateur nights" when talented nonprofessional entertainers competed for prizes.

It was on one of those amateur nights that I, bolstered by Rina, decided to go on stage and perform. What could I do? I certainly had no training of any sort. The things I did best would not have entertained the audience. But I knew a few songs by heart, and one of them seemed right for the occasion. We decided that I would enter the competition as a child singing star.

I was probably only about five years old at the time because I think I learned that particular song in kindergarten. At any rate, bursting with confidence I stood in line with the other hopeful performers. When my turn came, I walked on stage and started singing. "Every time the bubbles blow, rainbows come and go." Those are the only two lines I remember. Unfortunately, those were the only lines I remembered that night as well!

At first, forgetting the words didn't shake my confidence until I looked over the footlights and saw all those eyes focused on me. I sang the opening words loud and clear, and then I froze. I just stood there. The audience began to applaud immediately. They clapped and whistled until the master of ceremonies came and led me off the stage.

When it was time to pick the winner, all the performers, including me, were lined up on the stage, front and center. The audience was to be the judge. The emcee walked behind us and took turns putting his hand on our heads to invite applause. When he got to me, the audience went wild. The emcee tried to be fair because a few of the performers were talented semi-professionals and had put on

14

quite a show. That night they didn't stand a chance. There was nothing he could do but award first prize to me.

I wasn't the least embarrassed by what happened on stage. I couldn't help it if the audience thought I was good. Rina thought I was good! She was so proud of me. And although it was many, many years before I went on stage again, I was, and still am, permanently stage struck.

Chapter Two
Little Italian Angels

Looking back it is easy to find telltale signs of my Italian connection throughout my childhood. The most obvious is fierce loyalty. Like the Roman nose, intense loyalty is a prominent Italian feature. I suspect it was part of my personal profile from the very beginning. And I don't mean loyalty to a cause, or even a just cause, but rather loyalty just because. When I related to something or someone, it was forever. In English this is called stick-to-itiveness. In Italianese, it is known as Mafioso, which comes from the word mafia and rhymes with raffia involving the same interweaving and bonding. It might bend under pressure but almost never breaks.

My close ties with Rina were reinforced during those resilient summer months in Santa Cruz, but they never tied me down. What we didn't dare do alone, we devised a way to do together. Boredom was our mortal enemy. We were sisters. We could do no wrong. We had a reason for everything we did and it was always a good reason. Any reason was a good reason if it was ours. Not only were we full of ideas, but we had a rock-solid basis for every last one of them.   Perhaps I should preface this account of my childhood by saying that it is a testimony to my parents' ingenuity and hard work to realize that we were living through the tail end of the Great Depression without even knowing it. I always had the feeling of abundance. I was too proud and stubborn to ask for anything. I never failed to find a way to make do with what I had. Besides, Rina always found a way to get things for both of us. Because she suffered from childhood diseases, my parents indulged her beyond their means. I remember how Papa would put a $20 bill under her dinner plate to encourage her to eat. I suppose Anne and I had every reason to be jealous, but we weren't. I was as anxious for her to eat and be well as my parents were. I had put all my eggs in one basket so everything I did hinged on Rina.

Partly because of the special treatment she received, Rina developed a personality that wouldn't quit and a hot temper to go with it. She always got what she wanted. She knew when and how to explode. I loved her for that. I kept my real feelings hidden. She let them all hang out at the slightest provocation. She was a born fighter. She fought my battles as well as her own. No wonder I adored her unconditionally, even if she was "the favorite".

One of the typical battles I remember Rina fighting for me happened during a softball game on our block. All of the kids who lived on our street gathered in the late afternoon or early evening and turned one of the intersections into a playing field. I had no negative sense of racial consciousness and to me a race was something you ran, not a classification. We were all Americans, and in a softball game your standing was based on how well you could field a ball and swing a bat.

During one of our games, I was called "out" when I was sure I had touched the base before I was tagged. Rina went to my defense without question. She insisted that I was safe and picked up a bat challenging everyone to a fight. Rina was a runt, and some of the kids on our block were a lot older and bigger than she. When she saw that she was not only outnumbered but outweighed, she ran down the street and climbed her favorite tree, a huge English walnut just outside our driveway.

This tree was her fortress. She had defended it many times. She would climb just high enough so she could step on anyone's fingers who dared to try to follow her. She was wiry and quick. I never saw her lose a tree battle. After several attempts to dethrone her, even the biggest boys gave up and went back to playing softball. Rina had made her point. She was my big sister. Anyone who had a quarrel with me had to face her first.

Rina and I grew to be as thick as the proverbial thieves even though we each maintained close friends of our own. When we disliked someone, however, it was an all-out, mutual vendetta. For some reason, we couldn't stand the cousin of one of our friends who lived around the corner. Every time this cousin came to visit, we got stuck having to play with her. Somehow we had to get rid of her.

One of the games we played when we had nothing more exciting to do was "doctor". Since this unwanted visitor was on our turf, it was easy for us to insist that she had to be the patient all the time. This gave us authority to administer whatever "medicine" we happened to prescribe.

Our favorite prescription was a few spoonfuls of the crushed shells Mama fed the chickens. It was a high calcium supplement to grain that kept the eggs from cracking easily. It was also readily accessible. There was a big sack of it in the chicken house. It was awful stuff, almost impossible to swallow. Nevertheless, we made our unwilling patient eat it. She had no choice. If she wanted to play with us, and she did, then we were the doctor and the nurse, and she was the patient. Patients took the medicine the doctor prescribed, even if it was a bowl of crushed shells.

Before long we outgrew playing doctor. We were ready for bigger and better ideas, like making money. I, especially, was always looking for ways to get my hands on some. Rina had her own built-in source of income. All she had to do was refuse to eat and Papa would come through with a cash incentive. I didn't have that luxury so I came up with another idea.

When we were growing up kids were safe to roam the street freely, at least in a small city like St. Helena. On one of our outings, we noticed a row of beautiful rocks in the front garden of a rather nice house. We didn't know who lived there, but obviously they had good taste and liked beautiful things. So I picked up one of the rocks, cleaned off the dirt and walked around to the back door. Would the lady of the house like to buy a rock for her lovely garden? Of course, she did. How could she turn us down, two little girls with angelic faces? So she bought the rock and we were in business.

We walked all over town selling rocks. Usually we sold them to their owners, but once in a while we rearranged the landscaping here and there and sold them to any willing buyer. From rocks we progressed to flowers. We picked the flowers from someone's front yard and sold fresh, fragrant bouquets to the same owners at their back door.

One day we came home from an entrepreneurial foray and found our older sister, Anne, waiting for us. As I said before, Anne was not in our league. She never did anything wrong. Rina and I didn't think she did anything right, either. She just didn't _do_ anything. She wasn't full of ideas, like us. But there she was, our big sister, and she was waiting for us by the front gate.

21

Anne told us that the Chief of Police was coming to pick us up.

"What for?" we asked.

"For stealing," she said.

We didn't ask any questions. We had never thought of what we did as stealing. After all, we didn't really take anything away from any one. We gave them something that was theirs in the first place. If in turn they gave us money, we took it. That was all. You wouldn't expect us to turn down money, would you?

Anne made us sit on the steps on the front porch of our house and wait for the Chief of Police to arrive. As in most cases when someone has done something wrong, even if they did not know it was wrong at the time, there is a lesson to be learned. My conscience kicked in and so did Rina's. We sat there in silence and thought about what we had done. The more I thought, the more my self-pride suffered, realizing that I had taken advantage of someone else.

I grew up disliking anyone who took advantage of someone else. I remember Papa telling us how his sponsor had taken advantage of him when he came to the United

States. Because he could not read or speak English, Papa had been led to sign papers to work for fourteen years instead of seven to repay his sponsor. No doubt, the incident was motivated by racial prejudice, but Papa never took it that way. Even though he was still very much a foreigner, he thought of himself as an American. He could not imagine why someone from this land of overflowing opportunity would even think of taking advantage of anyone else. He loved being an American, a privilege he celebrated in a big way every Fourth of July.

I thought about Papa's experience as we sat on our front porch that day and waited to be taken to jail. I don't know how long we sat there, but it worked. Even though the police car never came, by late afternoon Rina and I had decided to go out of business. We certainly never suspected that Anne might have tricked us. I mean, there was no way Anne could have cooked up such a story by herself. Not our big sister, Anne. The Chief of Police must have just gotten too busy to come.

One of our favorite childhood projects was the redistribution of wealth. We noticed that some people had more than they needed while others did not have enough.

We took on the evangelical job of sharing the wealth, other people's wealth, of course.

In spite of the painful lesson we had learned a few weeks earlier in our business venture of selling rocks and flowers, we didn't see anything wrong with our new project. To us, it was wrong if you took something from someone else and kept it for yourself. We were going to take from those who had a lot and give to those who did not have enough. It was all so logical. Anything was logical if it kept us from being bored.

We had noticed that there were poor families living in the neighborhood who apparently couldn't afford to buy enough milk. In our town, the milk was delivered house to house by a Mr. Prouty. The milk was pasteurized but not homogenized. It came in glass quart bottles sealed with tight fitting caps that had little tabs on them. Mr. Prouty made his deliveries very late in the afternoon, so after school we could walk around and see at a glance how many bottles were left on each front porch. We knew who lived where, and if we saw a family with several children who didn't have what we thought was enough bottles lined up on their front porch, we took it upon ourselves to do something about it.

Our something was quite simple, and it was so logical. We took from those who had a lot and gave to those who had too few. Then we would go home feeling like little angels, little Italian angels.

Our angelic halos, like everything else about us, didn't last forever. One night we decided that those poor children needed the milk, all right, but they didn't need all the cream that rose to the top of each bottle. So we brought along a bowl and a spoon. Before we made our milk deliveries, we removed the caps carefully and spooned off just a dab or two of the cream. Both of us loved whipped cream, and the spoonfuls we took home were enough to whip up for desert that evening.

Where was our conscience, our sense of fairness, while this was going on? Apparently the lesson Ann taught us over selling rocks didn't stick. What did Mama and Papa think about our sudden supply of whipped cream? I honestly don't know. They were working long, long hours in their olive oil factory and the unexplained supply of cream got past them somehow. I do know they would have

25

been horrified had they been aware of our unorthodox welfare program.

What about Anne? Was she really that much of a dud? Didn't she wonder where we got the cream night after night? Again, I don't know. Like a witness on the stand, that is my only defense. I don't even know how long we did this, nor why we didn't suspect that Mr. Prouty, God rest his soul, would have had to replace the milk we carefully skimmed and delivered elsewhere. We were so self-confident in and for each other that it never occurred to Rina and me that any of our ideas could possibly have a downside.

Besides, we really liked Mr. Prouty, especially after he included a little note with his bill one month. The note was sent about the time that a group of religious zealots were going door to door alerting residents that the world was coming to an end, a big deal in the 1920's. Those of us who didn't repent would go straight to hell. Mr. Prouty's note was short on words and to the point:

"Please pay your bill on time. We don't want to run all over hell looking for you!

Chapter Three

Italian Revenge

Rina and I never seemed to have to run around to find things to do. One lazy summer day we discovered a new use for the tire pump Papa kept in the basement. We had a bicycle so we knew what the hand pump was for and how to use it. At that point, our Italian imagination took over.

I should preface this narration by admitting that I have a lifelong fascination with farting. I wish I could blame this fixation on my ethnic roots, but so far I have not found a legitimate or logical reason to do so. Farts have always tickled my fancy, that's all. They still do.

The idea came to us when we were using the hand pump to put air in our bike tires. To make the thing work well, we had to squat down and hold the nozzle firmly in place. A fart ensued. We put two and two together immediately and came up with a new use for the pump. We concluded that with it we should be able to produce bigger and better farts, and certainly more of them. It didn't take long for us to prove we were right.

We took turns, one manning the pump while the other pressed the outlet nozzle firmly in the right place. Oh, how we farted! We farted and giggled and farted some more. When Mama called us to go upstairs, we went up sounding like one-cycle motors. Fortunately, or perhaps unfortunately, we ran out of air before we got close enough to Mama for her to figure out what we had been up to.

That tire pump gave us a satisfying pastime we could fall back on whenever we were threatened with boredom. It is a wonder we didn't use it on one of our patients when we played doctor. For some unknown reason, we kept it strictly to and for ourselves. It was a bonus granted to us by our volatile Italian imagination.

This is not to say that other nationalities do not have active imaginations. I am sure they do. I am also sure that the Italian version has a perverse twist to it. There is something in our nature that enjoys a laugh at ourselves or at someone else's expense as long as it does not involve taking advantage. It means being ready to laugh if you see someone slip on a banana peel, especially if you are the one who put it there. Mama never knew what to expect next. For that matter, neither did we. New ideas just kept coming.

Mama had a friend who visited her once in a while and always managed to rub Rina and me the wrong way. She had a classy attitude, and the way she looked at us made us feel like toads. So, if she thought we were toads, we would prove she was right.

The lady drove her own car, unusual in those days, a Ford with a canvas top that bolted to the frame on both sides. While she was in the house exchanging pleasantries with Mama, we surveyed the car. There must be something we could do to it that would pay her back for being a snob. It had to be something that would happen after she drove off and couldn't be life threatening. We weren't that bad.

We put our heads together and came up with a plan. We would loosen the bolts that held the canvas top in place. The question was, how much should we loosen them? If the bolts were not loose enough, she could be out of town before the top blew off. If the bolts were too loose, the top might fall off while she was still in our driveway.

29

When the time came for the lady friend to leave, we stood beside Mama wearing our best halos. Mama eyed us suspiciously, but what could she say? We smiled demurely as we waved goodbye. The Ford rolled down our long driveway and out the gate. It had gone less than a block when the top blew off. The canvas-covered frame hovered airborne a moment before hitting the pavement and bucking like a horse. The lady jumped out of the car and threw up her hands trying to figure out what had happened. What a sight! It was a scene straight from the Keystone Cops.

Mama ran to help her friend put her precious Ford together again. We ran with her. We wouldn't have missed helping for the world. It took quite a bit of doing to get the bolts back in place. We waved happily when the lady finally drove off. Mama never reprimanded us in the presence of her friend. We knew that she knew we had something to do with what happened, but her sense of humor must have gotten the better of her. It was so funny and so unexpected. For the moment, she was on our side, right or wrong.

When we got home, however, Mama sat us down for a talk about manners. Rina listened meekly, and, to my surprise agreed with her. Playing a trick on that poor lady should not have been fun. I could see how Mama would say that, but I could not see how Rina didn't at least present our side of the case. Instead she nodded obediently while my fierce independence was fuming. After all, we were just having fun. The car was not damaged. It was the lady's pompous and superior attitude that had forced us to do what we did. If she had not put us down, we would not have had to put her in her place. She made us do it. By the end of Mama's talking-to, however, I reluctantly followed Rina's lead. I bowed to the rule that "Fun is fun when it is fun for everyone." At least for the moment.

If these stories give you a feeling that Rina was an important part of my childhood, you've got it right. She was my goddess, my Italian goddess. There is no way I can tell the story of my life and leave her out. Rina _was_ my childhood, my Italian sisterhood.

Almost all of the happy or important moments I remember as a child involved her. We shared everything. Yes, we had to share the same bedroom with Anne, but Rina and I shared the same bed, which to us became our own little world. We had a set of rules that each of us broke in typical Rina fashion, meaning, whenever we wanted. One of the rules was that unless we gave our permission, neither of us crossed over an imaginary line we drew down the middle of the mattress. This meant we could not touch each other without permission. If my toe accidentally touched hers, she had the right to give me a whack. And of course, the rule worked both ways. We stayed awake for hours defending our territory, all the while loving each other with fierce possessiveness.

Anne would look across the room at us in disgust, totally unable to understand why we didn't just stop provoking each other and go to sleep. Go to sleep when we were having so much fun? Go to sleep when you could hold your finger so close to the other one's eye that she couldn't blink without touching it? Our game of touch and whack went on until far past our bedtime. Then we curled up together like a pair of kittens and woke up bright-eyed and ready for a new adventure. We played hard, but we loved harder.

Rina and I shared a bike, a single speed two-wheeler that we each enjoyed as a way to cruise the neighborhood. Sometimes we would ride it at the same time, but not in the usual way kids do, with the extra person sitting on the handlebars or behind the seat. We both wanted to pedal, so we each got on one side of the bike and used our inside legs to pedal with, leaving the outside leg to hang loose. Then we crossed arms to hold the handlebars and away we went. We rode all over town this way, dodging cars and other cyclists.

All went well until one day we came to a corner where Rina wanted to stay on the road while I wanted to go on the sidewalk. She pulled her way and I pulled my way and we ran smack into a huge telephone pole. The front wheel collapsed under the impact. We were thrown up in the air, Rina just missing the oncoming traffic and me just missing being impaled on an iron picket fence. But it was fun!

Another "fun" thing we did in those airhead days was to put on skates and convince an older teenager we knew into letting us hang on to the back of his car while he drove down the highway. We only did this at night, of course. There was not so much traffic then and the headlights warned us of an approaching car. How fast did we go? I don't think we asked, but it was never fast enough.

Even when the sparks would fly from the metal wheels of our skates, curiosity drove us to see if we could go faster, to push the outer limits of experience as far as we possibly could.

In relating incidents like this I am admitting to what airheads we were. We never stopped to think of what it would do to our parents financially if we were seriously hurt, since that was a distinct possibility considering the speed we attained and the poor visibility at night. We loved our parents and knew they were not wealthy. We had heard how they came to be US citizens and the struggle they had to just make a living. Still, we never gave them a thought. We were having fun. You don't think when you are having fun. I hope that the parents who read this impress this point on the children in their care. I also hope young readers will remember this before they put themselves and their parents in jeopardy by pushing the envelope too far. How far is too far? When there is a good chance that you could be crippled for life and burden your family with the endless responsibility of caring for an invalid child; that is going too far.

Chapter Four

Having Fun

As I grew older, I eventually learned that through books I could satisfy my curiosity about things without having to experience them myself. On this point, Rina and I differed. She hated to read and I loved to. This gave her an excuse to make special use of her little sister. Every time one of the teachers assigned a book for her to read, Rina brought it home to me. I not only had to read it, but I wrote the book report for her. It was a happy arrangement for both of us. I was getting a wide range of literary experience way ahead of my years and Rina was getting away with something, which to her was always a pleasant experience.

One day she came home from school and told me that I had to write a book. I objected on the grounds that that was asking a bit much of me. Besides, I didn't know how to go about writing a whole book. I didn't even know where to start.

"But you write all the time!" she argued.

She was right. The massive reading I was doing stirred my creative juices. As a result, I had started writing stories on my own, not just doing her reports. Still, a book sounded like a formidable project and I continued to object. Rina's confidence in me finally drove me to agree to do it for her.

I always loved poetry, so I worked on a series of poems which she could compile into a book. Once I got started, the writing just flowed. In a short time I had enough pages for her to turn in.

I gave the manuscript the title of "Have You Seen The Butter Fly?" This set the theme for the text, using a witty sense of common words to spark the reader's imagination. From a literary standpoint, it was not well done. But it had a few clever bits, my favorite being, "Have you see an ant elope?" which was no more ridiculous than seeing butter fly.

She copied the manuscript word for word and gave it to her teacher well ahead of schedule. To this day, I can't see what any teacher saw in those poems. In my judgment, they are awful. I am embarrassed by them, but Rina loved them and so did the teacher. She liked them so well that she shared them with the rest of the faculty. Eventually, they were made into a book complete with a title page and the name of the author, which was, of course, Rina's name, not mine.

When I share this story with school children on my Author Festival visits, they always ask why I didn't tell on Rina? Why didn't I at least tell my mother? To tell on Rina was the last thing I would have done. Even now it is not easy to explain my relationship with my sister, how she owned me. Sometimes I qualify that statement by admitting that we really owned each other. I get a warm feeling when I watch young siblings interacting, the older one always insisting on being in charge. I think, how fortunate they are to be part of an all-encompassing sisterhood such as we had.

As close as we were, Rina and I managed to get into trouble separately as well as together. My most regretful habit was stealing, or rather, borrowing cars. I can't account for what I did except to say that I was full of zest, Italian zest, and since I couldn't afford a Ferrari of my own, I took whatever was handy.

I wasn't given the chance to learn to drive like Rina, in the safety of our driveway with parental supervision, which I tell about later. As a matter of fact, I didn't learn to drive. I just drove. Borrowing cars was one of the first things I did entirely on my own initiative. When I was with Rina, she was always the leader, the one in command. When I was on my own or with a girlfriend, I began to assume the role of leader.

I was barely eleven years old when I suggested to a girlfriend that we borrow a car and take it for a spin. The idea came to me one evening when we were walking past a row of parked cars on Main Street on our way home from playing in the school yard. I noticed that most of the cars had the keys left in the ignition. In a small town such as ours, that was not uncommon. The drivers were enjoying a drink in one of the bars and were in no hurry to go home. Neither were we in a hurry, so why not do something exciting?

Before we could change our minds, we picked out a car and got in. I turned on the key. The engine responded instantly and we were in business. I had paid careful attention when Papa gave Rina her driving lessons at home so I knew what the procedure was, especially the importance of shifting carefully and smoothly when changing gears. Let the clutch out slowly, and at the same time step on the gas just enough to get moving. On my first try, I found reverse gear and we roared back out of the parking space without snapping off our heads. Then I shifted into low, and with pounding hearts and a few healthy jerks we were off.

I turned off Main Street and headed for the back roads. It was the most exciting thing I had ever even imagined doing. Once we were out in the countryside, my girlfriend begged for a turn to drive. I pulled to a stop and we changed seats. She had not had vicarious driving lessons like me, so it took quite a few tries, stalled motors, and severe jerks before we were on our way again.

She was just getting the hang of steering when we saw a car coming our way. The back road we were on was narrow, with hardly enough room for cars to pass each other. The worse part was that at the speed we were going, the two cars coming from opposite directions would meet at a sharp bend in the road where there was a culvert and a fairly deep ditch on either side.

At the last minute, my girlfriend panicked and let loose of the steering wheel. At the same time, her foot involuntarily hit the gas pedal. We lurched forward. I grabbed the wheel and somehow from the passenger's seat managed to steer the car around the bend without hitting the oncoming vehicle.

The look on the other driver's face convinced me that we had pushed our luck far enough. I got into the driver's seat and we headed back to town. We parked the car in the same place where we found it, grabbed our jackets out of the back seat and ran all the way to my house without looking back.

When we were almost there, we sprawled on the curb and rested while we caught our breath. Then we looked at each other and all at once realized what we had done. We started laughing in sheer relief. Before heading for home, we swore not to tell another soul. I never told anyone, but once I knew I could drive, I couldn't wait to get behind the wheel of a car again.

After that, when ever I saw a car with the key left in the ignition, I tried to make fairly sure the owner would be gone long enough for me to take it for a spin, and off I went, mostly alone, mostly under cover of darkness, sort of daring myself to see if I could get away with it. I loved being independent, a trait that is as Italian as it is American, and driving a car gave me that feeling of freedom.

I was so independent, in fact, that when I was twelve years old I decided I didn't want my parents to have to buy my clothes any longer. I wanted to be able to buy them myself. So I went out and got a job as a maid in a wealthy household even though I knew none of the finer points of manners and etiquette that the job required. I lasted just two weeks before getting laid off. Being fired didn't discourage me from looking for other employment, and very shortly going to work for the Chief of Police, of all people, to do the cooking for his family.

When I applied for that job, I admitted that I knew nothing about preparing meals, but that I was willing to learn. I wrote the Chief's wife a note telling her of my total lack of experience but assuring her that I would be prompt, clean and efficient, that I could follow orders and wasn't afraid to work hard. Oh yes, and I also wanted twice the pay of the girl I was replacing and three days off before I could start! The Chief's wife told me later that they hired me because they thought any young girl that gutsy ought to have a chance to prove herself. And I did. I made a success of the job and worked for them for a number of years.

Chapter Five
Satisfying Curiosity

Working for the Chief of Police gave me the advantage of knowing if the law was closing in on our pranks. By that time, in addition to all our crazy schemes, Rina was in high school and had started drinking with her friends. We had wine at the dinner table every night and Papa encouraged us to have a glass with our meal. To him, it was perfectly natural and Rina enjoyed the social rite of passage. I couldn't stand the stuff. I was, and am, a confirmed milk drinker. I am the ideal candidate for one of those "Got milk?" ads. I learned to cook with wine when I was an adult and worked for a time as a chef, but I never learned to like the taste of fermented grape juice. More importantly, I definitely disliked what it did to me. Drinking made me light headed instantly. It made me feel as if I were on the verge of losing self-control. Being a

"Miss Independence", that was enough for me to avoid alcohol like the plague.

With Rina, drinking was a social thing and bolstered her feeling that life was a party so live it up. She didn't drink a lot, but it didn't take much to get her drunk enough to be vulnerable. I hated that with a passion. I would be furious with whoever supplied her with alcohol and immediately became the big sister determined to protect her. We went dancing here and there several nights a week, usually going together although we often separated during the evening. If Rina took a drink, she knew I would come looking for her, so she tried to hide from me. I would get someone to take me with them and drive from one dance hall to the other until I found her.

One night I couldn't find her anywhere. I was getting madder and more worried by the minute. Finally someone tipped me off that she had been seen at a nearby dance hall. I went there as soon as I could find a ride. She wasn't on the dance floor, so I decided to check the women's lounge. There were a number of girls milling around the room but none of them said a word. I got the uneasy feeling from their sheepish looks that something was wrong, so instead of leaving, I checked all the stalls. Still no Rina. Then I saw a puff of brown curls sticking up from behind the oversized trash can. Sure enough, there she was.

When she knew that I saw her, she drew herself up as tall as she could and ordered in a big voice, "Don't you touch me! I'm your big sister!"

Not that night, she wasn't! I picked her up, threw her over my shoulder like a sack of potatoes, and carried her across the middle of the dance floor. She pounded my back with her fists and protested angrily, "Put me down! I'm your big sister!" The crowd of dancers loved it. They gave us room to get by and a round of applause as I carried her out the door and into the waiting car. She knew she couldn't fight me. Her little sister had grown to be bigger and stronger than she was. I still looked up to Rina even though at times I had to look down to do so.

Despite our wild ways, Rina and I managed to make it through puberty without gaining much sexual experience. There were a few minor incidents, but we had devised a system of warning that worked for us. It was so simple that it can be described in one word, "rock". When either of us

45

suspected that a boy had something on his mind other than altruistic fun, we would say "rock". Immediately the other one knew that something was up, and it wasn't necessarily a healthy up.

The boys in our neighborhood never treated us like girls, so our opinion of boys was based mostly on those we met through our parents' circle of friends. These boys had the usual run-of-the-mill mentality that thought they were better than us because they had a penis. We relied on our code word, "rock", to warn us when the gleam in their eyes was horny. It did not, however, protect us from the other function the penis served: peeing, to be exact.

One of our parents' well-to-do friends was in the artichoke business and had a huge warehouse where the freshly-picked produce was stored. We must have been between five to seven years old when we were invited there for a visit. Their son was a few years older than us and a number of tricks wiser, at least where a penis was concerned. That afternoon he lured us into an empty section of the warehouse where he managed to climb up on the rafters. The room was dark when we entered. The next thing we knew, we were being showered with a vile-smelling liquid we recognized instantly as urine. Rina and I were furious and planned to make him one of our special concoctions, which I will leave to the reader's imagination, as soon we got home. We never got around to it, but that was the one and only time he got the better of us.

I can't remember the boy's name, but I've never forgotten the sheer volume and repulsive warmth of that unexpected shower. In fact, only once in my life have I seen anyone out-urinate him, and it was an amazing little five-year-old girl. I was taking her and her older sister and twin younger brothers for a walk in the woods one afternoon when we came upon a small canyon. Immediately, the twins, who were about four years old, whipped out their penises and showed us girls how far they could jettison a stream. Before I could react, the younger sister squatted down and let fly a stream of urine that outdid her brothers by a good six feet! Somehow, her astonishing feat avenged my soul for that degrading shower in the warehouse years before when I was about her age.

Being brought up in a family of girls, my curiosity about penises in general was whetted by the few brief glimpses I had had of the male plumbing while watching a diaper being changed. I decided I wanted to see the real thing "up front and close". For some reason, Rina wasn't interested. She had probably already explored that forbidden territory on her own and had avoided telling me. At any rate, I wanted to see for myself.

One evening I managed to sneak into my parents' bedroom and hide under the bed. I have no idea how I planned to get out of the room without them finding me. I didn't think that far ahead. Consequences were not part of my mental process. So there I was under the bed when Papa came into the room and shut the door behind him. I wasn't sure if Lady Luck was shining on me, or if he had spotted my presence and was going to confront me. I held my breath and waited.

Everything was quiet for a moment, and then the bedsprings creaked. That meant Papa had sat down on the edge of the bed. Off came his shoes, one by one. Then he stood up and dropped his pants. I rolled over slowly, just far enough so I could look up without being seen. The light from the bedroom lamp wasn't the brightest, but it was good enough for me to see all I wanted to see. Papa was well endowed. I guess his ample endowment had what is known as "crotch itch". His remedy was an alcohol rub which he proceeded to give himself, leaping and gasping as the stinging got to him. The scene was almost too much for me, a full-grown penis with appendages doing a tarantella right before my eyes. So much for my curiosity about penises.

Chapter Six
Rina's Temper

One of Rina's distinguishing traits was her explosive temper. It was as much a part of my Italian childhood as of hers, but not to the same degree. Every once in a while she would turn her temper on me, although that never affected our sisterhood one bit. Her outbursts were like a display of fireworks. You never knew for sure where or when the sparks were going to fly. And if a few of them landed on me, well, that was life. In that sense, we did our share of living.

Once in a great while when we were in our teens, Mama and Papa would leave for a day and give us chores to do. On one such occasion, Papa killed a chicken before he left and we were given the task of plucking it. He had everything set up for us. There was a small gas stove in the shed and a big kettle we could use to boil the water. There was also a convenient outdoor work area with running water, a cutting board, knives, a deep pail and an array of kitchen utensils.

To the digital generation, this probably sounds like ancient history, but there was a time not too long ago when you didn't go to the supermarket to buy a supply of meat. If you wanted a chicken, you didn't pluck a wrapped package out of a glass case. You bought the fowl live, took it home and killed and dressed it.

In case you have never plucked a chicken and don't know what is involved, let me explain that you start by scalding the carcass with boiling water so the feathers can be pulled out. We had seen Papa do this many times, but now I guess he figured we were old enough to do it ourselves. Remember, he grew up in Italy so to him it wasn't such an unreasonable thing to expect of us. Besides, Anne must have been about sixteen by then since she was six years older than me. It was up to the three of us to figure out a way to scald the dead fowl and not scald ourselves.

While we were trying to decide what to do, Rina assumed the role of director of operations. She insisted that we should hold the dead chicken by its feet and dunk it into the pail filled with boiling water. Anne and I argued that we should put the chicken in the pail feet first and pour the water over it. Our reasoning was that it would be easier to skin the feet doing it our way. Yes, the feet had to be skinned. Eventually, they went into the soup pot, Italian style, meaning you didn't waste anything. I speak from experience. Skinning the feet of a dead chicken is a distasteful task if ever there was one.

The water came to a boil before we had resolved the question of which came first, the chicken or the hot water. Rina started barking orders at us. Anne and I refused to obey. That did it. Rina blew her fuse. She began to throw things and we began to laugh. That was the ultimate mistake on our part. The more we laughed, the more she threw, starting with the dead chicken, the large pail, the cutting board and knives, and finally the kettle of boiling water.

Anne and I had learned to be pretty good at dodging, so we managed to survive the onslaught while Rina stormed off, leaving us with the mess. I don't remember if we ever got the chicken plucked before Mama and Papa got home, but I know we didn't tell on Rina. She might get mad all over again, and who knows what she would do?

On another occasion, the three of us were in the kitchen pantry cleaning vegetables for dinner. The pantry had a sink and a long counter, so there was ample room for us to work without getting in each other's way. This was important, because the vegetables had to be prepared just so.

Papa had been a chef and still did all the cooking. He was extremely fussy about the appearance of the dishes he served. Even if the vegetables were only going into a stew, the visual effect had to be appealing to the eye. The carrots must be peeled and cut into slender fingers. The celery must be snapped to remove the strings before it was cut into one-inch crescents. Finally the new potatoes and onions were cubed so they could be arranged in the gravy to create an appetizing pattern. At the last minute, freshly shelled peas and finely chopped Italian parsley would be sprinkled on top for color accent.

As usual, Rina was in charge. I don't know why Anne never was. As the oldest sister, she had the authority. I suppose she just didn't want to risk an argument. Anne was definitely one of those who would rather switch than fight, a trait foreign to our Italian genes.

We had half of the vegetables done when something didn't go exactly as Rina thought Papa wanted. Instead of just explaining, she started yelling and waving her arms at us. She became so violent so suddenly that Anne and I began to snicker. We tried not to, but Rina heard us and the fireworks began. Anne and I backed out of the pantry as quickly as we could, followed by handfuls of carrot fingers, celery crescents, and potato and onion cubes. Next Rina gathered the vegetable brush, the cutting board, and the knives and let them fly. The piece de resistance was the dishpan full of water. She had a pretty good arm, so the water spattered the entire kitchen. Off she stormed, leaving Anne and me to mop up.

Rina's temper kept the whole family on its toes. One afternoon she came home from school ranting and raving. She had been involved in a hands-on fight with a classmate who was older and bigger than her. Somehow, as petite as she was, she managed to get a strangle hold on the girl. We were sitting around the kitchen table listening to her describe the incident in detail. The more she talked, the

54

more excited she got. Before Papa could defend himself, she grabbed him around the neck and demonstrated the kind of strangle hold she had used. By the time he pulled her arms loose, his eyeballs were bulging. I mean, how could the rest of us help but laugh? She was our main source of daily entertainment.

When Rina decided she wanted to learn to drive the car, Papa agreed to teach her the basics and let her practice in our driveway. The garage was at the far end of our property. Rina could start the car and back straight out of the garage, veer slightly to the left, then continue past the house all the way to the gate. There she would turn the car around and practice parking before driving back. She did this over and over, invariably with Papa sitting besides her and me in the back seat cheering her on.

Papa was in the olive oil business so when the olives were ripe he hired pickers to help harvest the crop. Papa was not easy to work for. In fact, as a boss he was impossible. He was far too quick and efficient for anyone to keep up with him. His workers were constantly walking off the job and having to be replaced.

Early one morning Papa had two new workers waiting to be transported to the olive orchard. Rina asked if she could back the car out of the garage, a routine she knew by heart. Papa agreed and got into the front seat beside her. The two workmen got in the back seat. I went upstairs to the second story porch where I had a ringside seat to watch my sister perform.

Rina started the car and somehow did something that Papa didn't think was quite right. He criticized her, gently but firmly. Rina told him in no uncertain terms to leave her alone. She knew what she was doing. She could back out of the garage with her eyes closed. Papa tried to explain that he was still in charge even though she was sitting in the driver's seat. His words lit Rina's fuse. Just like that, she screamed at him to leave her alone.

Papa shouted back, "Get out of the car this minute!"

"Not until I back out of the garage like you said I could!" Rina cried, her face distorted with rage.

By then, Papa's fuse was lit, too. "I will tell you what you can do!" he ordered.

"I will *show* you what I can do!" Rina countered.

With that, she put the car in reverse and stepped on the gas. The car shot out of the garage at full speed and slammed straight into the corner of the house.

It was another of our family's Keystone Cops episode. The front doors flew open. Rina and Papa jumped out and faced each other in a screaming match. At the same time, the back doors flew open and out came the workers. They didn't wait to see who won the argument. They raced down the long driveway and out the gate. The last I saw of them, they were still running.

Family album

Our parents' wedding

Anne with me as an infant

At home

The three sisters

Big sis Anne with me

Rina and me with cats

Rina

Anne as a teenager

Me as a teenager

"Seniors' sneak"

Our parents' 25th wedding anniversary

Chapter Seven
Frog Paranoia

In spite of her temper, or maybe because of it, Rina was by far the family pet. Nevertheless because I was much taller than my sisters and had good physical ability, I became my father's surrogate son. Mama said that when I was born, making him the father of three girls, he held me in his arms and sang, "Beneditto fra le donne!" which was his facetious version of the angel's pronouncement to Mary in the Bible, "Blessed art thou among women." Fortunately I grew up to be tomboy enough to satisfy his need for masculine activities.

I was still quite young, possibly nine or ten years old, when he bought a gun for me, a rifle, and taught me to use it. I became such a good shot that he took me with him to a ranch where a group of men had a target shooting range. It wasn't long before I was good enough to compete with the best of them. Papa was so proud of me. He was a marksman and it pleased him no end that I was carrying on in his footsteps.

One winter morning I got up while everyone else was still in bed and stood on our back porch watching the driving rain whip the branches of our huge walnut tree. The bare branches swung back and forth somewhat like the moving targets the men used on the shooting range. A small bird landed on the tip of one of the branches and clung there while the wind whipped it back and forth. As I watched, I thought what an impossible target the bird made. Without intending to use it, I loaded my rifle and went outside and stood on the top step under the overhanging roof.

It never occurred to me for a moment that I could hit the bird since the tree was a good distance away from the porch steps. Besides, strong gusts of wind were making me sway back and forth as well as the tree. Everything was blowing about in a constant, erratic motion with no rhythm to it. I was fascinated and kept my eye trained on that tiny target. Suddenly I knew that I could do it. Forgetting that it was a live bird and not a clay or glass target, I pulled the trigger. The bird fell to the ground.

Actually, it didn't fall to the ground. It landed in a puddle of water formed by the runoff from the garage roof. The tiny creature fluttered helplessly trying to keep its head above water. I had an emotional melt-down. I didn't have the courage to try to rescue the bird, so I did the only thing possible. I screamed for Papa.

If there is anything I could not stand as a child and still cannot stand, it is to see an animal suffer. Human suffering is different. I once helped a doctor suture a split scalp without flinching, but I will go to great lengths to avoid killing a fly or a spider. So there I was, the cause of that little bird's deathly struggle, and unable to do anything but scream for Papa.

Papa came all right, but when he saw what my blood curdling screams were about, he turned and went right back to bed. How ridiculous could I get? Why worry about a bird? At least if it was big enough to eat it might be worth retrieving, but this one wouldn't even make a mouthful. I was left standing there alone, transfixed by the last feeble efforts of the wounded fledgling to save itself.

I never touched my rifle again. Papa could argue and reason all he wanted. I was through with guns. The brilliant career as a marksman he envisioned for me was down the drain.

That incident stands out very clearly as a milestone in my eventual decision to become a vegetarian. It was not the first time I came face to face with the conflict between my need to eat versus my reverence for all living things. As a very young child I had terrible nightmares involving animal suffering. In spite of being daring and adventurous, I had an active conscience. I blamed myself ruthlessly when I saw any living creature suffer, especially if I could do nothing about it. Time and again I watched Papa kill something for our dinner. Each time, part of me deep inside died with it. With each chicken whose head he chopped off, each bird he trapped, each pig that was bled to death to make blood sausage, each rabbit whose neck he broke, I suffered a wave of overwhelming panic from which there was no escape.

To make matters worse, I never said anything to anyone about my feelings. I never even told Rina. I didn't think she would understand and would consider it a sign of weakness. I knew if I said something. I would be ridiculed. Nobody else in the family seemed to care. We ate meat, didn't we? How else could we eat it unless something was killed? The horns of that dilemma had me. But not forever. I was an adult before the realization dawned one day that I didn't have to eat meat if I didn't want to. I stopped just like that, and so did the turmoil in my mind. Why hadn't I thought of it sooner? Why hadn't I told Rina how I felt? It was a point I had to come to by myself, for myself, totally on my own terms as a conscious being.

I would like to relate one of the particularly terrifying experiences I had because of Papa's old-world means of putting meat on the table. It is the low point in my Italian childhood and has to do with frogs.

Frog hunting is an especially horrendous thing to watch. Our whole family would go to a river some place, as peaceful a setting as you can imagine. Then Papa and his men friends would tie large forks to the ends of long poles. By using them as pitchforks, they could reach into the depth of the quiet pools and spear the frogs in mid-leap if necessary. The impaled frogs didn't die. They were pulled off the forks and dropped into a sack. When enough of them had been caught, the sack was brought home and taken to the basement where the frogs' heads were cut off.

I can see them now. The eyes kept right on blinking. The legs kept right on jumping. In fact, they even jumped after they were in the frying pan. How many nightmares I had over those frogs! How many times I was awakened by the feeling of a frog clawing my hand!

Eventually something humorous came out of my frog paranoia. It happened years later when we had the campground at Anchor Bay and I was walking our St. Bernard dogs on the beach. The children staying in the campground lined up twice a day to take turns coming with me to take them on a run. Early one morning it was Patti and Mickie's turn. When we got to the far end of the cove, we would release the dogs so they could run ahead and swim in the surf while we followed at our own pace, picking up litter as we went. Keeping the beach clean was one of my passions.

I had picked up a discarded beer can, one of those tall thin ones, and was swinging it in my hand as we walked. Suddenly I felt fingers pressing against my palm. I dismissed the feeling as an illusion. Patti and Mickie were the only other people on the beach and they were about two feet away on either side of me. Then I felt those fingers squeezing my hand again. This time I looked down. A big lizard was starting to crawl out of the beer can I was holding, using his claws on the back of my hand for traction.

My reaction was instant and all-out. I threw the can into the air and started screaming and running around in circles, stamping my feet and trying to rid myself of the feel of those frog-like claws gripping my hand. Patti and Mickie were stunned. One minute we were chatting away relaxed and happy and the next I was having hysterics.

"What's the matter? What's the matter?" they kept asked frantically.

I couldn't say a word. All I could do was run around in circles screaming, trying to distance myself from the image of a basement full of headless frogs. It was obvious to my young companions that I was trying to escape from something, but there was nothing anywhere near me. About then, the St. Bernards heard my voice and came running, soaking wet with sea water. They thought I was playing some kind of a game and wanted to join in. They jumped on me and knocked me down, then proceeded to wrestle with me and each other in the sand. They were barking as loudly as I was screaming. The whole scene was out of control. Patti and Mickie were about to run back and get help when I managed to force one word out of my throat, "LIZZZZZARD!"

Immediately Patti and Mickie figured out what had happened.

They pulled off the dogs and helped me to my feet. I was quite a mess. One of them found the beer can, and sure enough the lizard had crawled back as far inside as it could get. For Patti and Mickie to see me act that way over a lizard was totally unexpected. This was not the Olga they knew. I should have told them about my childhood experience with frogs, but they were laughing too hard for me to spoil their fun. I just laughed with them, glad that I could find humor in what had been a nightmare for me for so long.

Chapter Eight

To Wed or Not To Wed

The tendency to laugh under stress has a particular affinity to being Italian. I guess affability is common to other ethnic groups, but with Italians it is uncommonly common. Italians laugh at all costs. When I think of my childhood, I always laugh. When our family gets together, we laugh. We laugh when someone trips and falls. We laugh at funerals, when it is the last thing we should be doing.

Mama's funeral was no exception. By then, we were no longer children. We were grown up and heartbroken, but we laughed. Under the stress of grief, it didn't take much to get us started. All it took was a manufacturer's label dangling from the suit jacket of one of the pallbearers. The poor man evidently went to the expense of buying a new suit for the occasion. Somehow, the label was not removed.

It was attached just low enough to get trapped in his crotch where it flip-flopped back and forth as he walked.

Rina, Anne, Papa and I were following the solemn procession bearing Mama's casket down the center aisle of the church when we spotted the wagging label. It triggered an involuntary giggle. We glanced at each other and began to convulse. Thank God our eyes were tearful and our hankies handy. We lowered our heads and dabbed at our faces. As soon as we were out of the church, we made a beeline for the waiting limousine, climbed inside and closed the doors. With the curtains pulled, we burst out laughing.

The hysterics lasted all the way to the burial site. I don't know what the driver thought, but as we stepped out of the limousine I heard people comment on how hard we must have been crying to have such red faces and tear-filled eyes.

Mama's untimely death ended a marital relationship that was a constant source of joy for my sisters and me. She and Papa made a remarkable couple, especially considering how their wedding came about. I love that story. I had Papa tell it many times. Whether or not I appreciated it when I was growing up, their relationship was the warp and weft of my Italian childhood. It still is.

When Papa Orlando was a young man, he was given the opportunity to pay for his passage to California by working for whoever sponsored him. He couldn't wait to get to the land of opportunity. He left behind him in Italy his devilish youth and perpetual hunger. Once he got here, he settled down to the business of life in a new country. He worked hard for twice the prescribed seven years to pay back his passage. Finally he was on his own. He made his way up and down the coast earning a living with and without his accordion. He was adventurous and easily bored, so he didn't stay long in one place. He did all kinds of work, including working on a dairy farm. That job meant that twice a day at milking time he could fill up on rich, warm milk directly from the cows. He told me that was the first time in his entire life that he could remember not being hungry.

Papa was in San Francisco when the 1906 earthquake shook the city to its core. He said that he was jolted out of his bed and rushed out to the street to review the damage. Almost immediately, he was recruited to help with the clean up. I have a tape recording of him telling about the experience and his voice is heavy with emotion as he describes having to haul dead bodies and watching the soldiers deliberately light fires on Van Ness Avenue to stop the advancing flames. As soon as he could get away, he left San Francisco and went as far south as San Diego, working at whatever job he could find. Eventually he bought a hotel in St. Helena, the heart of the Napa Valley wine country. He became the chef and indulged in what became his life-long affair with food.

The biggest problem Papa faced as the chef of his own hotel was that good help was hard to find. Even as a young man he was a bear to work for, or to work with, so his waitresses quit regularly. His friends had a suggestion. Why not get married, and then he would have kitchen help that would not walk out on him? Papa's first reaction was to scoff at the idea. Finally, his problem with hired help got so bad it drove him to agree that getting married might be the lesser of two evils.

His friends knew of a young Italian woman who worked at the Ghiradelli chocolate factory in San Francisco. She was single and beautiful, which in their minds meant that she was looking for a mate. Her name was Filomena Micheli. These friends arranged a meeting between Orlando and Filomena. They accompanied him to the city to make sure he didn't back out. At the initial meeting a formal marriage proposal was discussed and tentatively agreed upon. At a second meeting the details were worked out and the agreement finalized. They would see each other for the third time and exchange vows in San Francisco on April 19, 1913.

Papa had a few weeks to stew over his coming marriage. Should he or shouldn't he go through with it? It was not an easy decision, but his waitresses kept quitting and good help seemed impossible to find. The choice was his to make, and it was clear-cut. Give up being a chef or get married. He wasn't ready for the former, so he bought a new suit of clothes and prepared for the inevitable.

Early on the morning of April 19th, Papa got dressed and went downstairs to catch the stagecoach southbound to San Francisco. At the last minute, he panicked.

"What am I doing?" he asked himself. "I don't want to get married. I just want some good help in the kitchen. I

78

must have been crazy to let those fellows talk me into this!" He decided to go dancing instead. Back upstairs he went.

He took off his new suit and put on comfortable sports clothes. He would catch the northbound stagecoach and go to Middletown, one of his favorite resorts. Papa loved to dance and Middletown wasn't too far from St. Helena. He would spend the day indulging himself.

As soon as he had changed clothes, Papa dashed downstairs, just in time to see the one and only stagecoach already past the hotel on its way north through town. So he went upstairs again and got back into his wedding suit. A short while later he caught the southbound coach for San Francisco. This is how Orlando and Filomena came to be our parents.

I would have loved to know the details of how their marriage was consummated that night. Neither of them ever offered to tell us anything about it. When we were bold enough to ask, they looked at each other and smiled knowingly. We were left to imagine how these two strong individuals with such different backgrounds and outlooks eventually came to terms with each other and bonded for life.

Mama had been on her own since she was orphaned at the age of twelve. She had two younger sisters who were put in the care of a convent, and two brothers. One of them was sent to South America to live and the other in time came to California. Her father, my grandfather whom I never knew, made three trips to "America" on a sailboat before settling down in Italy. He even kept diaries of those trips. Mama remembered reading them, although she never knew what became of them. As a writer, I mourned the loss of those treasured accounts many times over the years. I've wondered what impressions this forefather thought worthy of recording for posterity.

When friends of the family arranged her passage to the United States, Mama found herself in San Francisco and was given a job at Ghiradelli's, famous for its chocolates. I recall her saying how she had always loved a chocolate bar, a rare treat for her in Italy. After a few months at the factory, her taste for them was completely gone. Perhaps I inherited that aversion, because it is the one flavor I can tolerate only if I have a big glass of milk to go with it and a chaser of sourdough bread.

Mama's life as an orphan in Italy had been hard. One of her responsibilities was to cut and haul grass for the livestock, walking miles to gather fresh armloads every day. She was in the third grade when her parents died and her formal schooling ended. Nevertheless, she was intellectually quick. When it came to math, she was brilliant. She could solve my high school algebra and trigonometry problems with ease, and calculus was a natural exercise for her mind.

Mama didn't need higher education while she was in Italy. She needed physical stamina to do the chores that fell on her young shoulders. Along with everything else, it was up to her to grow flax so she and her younger sisters could weave cloth for the family's needs. I still have a few of those precious linens, some with meticulously hand-stitched initials. The bed sheets, especially, I use frequently, not to put on our beds, but as tablecloths for our over-sized dining room table. The linen has lost much of its coarseness over the years, but none of its intrinsic value. I look forward to sharing these reminders of Mama's life with my grandchildren.

One of my favorite stories about Orlando and Filomena took place when they moved to a ranch in the mountains above Napa valley. After a few successful years, Papa had become bored with the hotel and was ready for a new challenge. A ranch sounded like just the thing. So they left the comforts and financial security of the hotel in St. Helena for the harsh reality of farming on Hall Mountain.

The very first morning on the ranch, Papa couldn't wait to go out and start working the virgin soil. Before he left, Mama asked him about dinner. This would be the first time she was to cook for them. At the hotel, the kitchen was his domain. Mama had learned a lot just watching him even though he had always insisted on doing the cooking entirely by himself.

"Tell me what you want me to fix for dinner," she said as Papa strode out the door.

"Cook whatever you feel like," Papa replied and was gone.

He returned at dinner time hungry as the proverbial bear. "What are we having for dinner?" he asked.

"Minestrone," Mama said. It had taken hours to prepare the vegetables just the way he liked them for this quintessential Italian soup.

"Oh," Papa sighed. "All day my mouth watered for polenta."

Mama said nothing, but the next morning as he rushed outside she asked him again, "Now tell me what you want me to fix for dinner."

Papa had his mind on other things. "Cook whatever you want," he muttered and again was gone.

So Mama fixed polenta and chicken with a wine-tomato sauce using his favorite seasonings.

Come dinnertime and Papa burst into the kitchen asking, "What are we having for dinner?"

"Polenta with chicken," Mama announced proudly.

"Oh," sighed Papa, "I have been thinking of roast pork all day, with new potatoes on the side".

Mama held her tongue, but right then and there she made up her mind. Tomorrow she would demand that he tell her exactly what he wanted to eat.

Morning came, and for the third time Mama asked about dinner. Papa was impatient with the nagging question. "Cucina un fischio!" he snapped as he hurried out the door. Literally, his words mean to cook a whistle, but figuratively they are equivalent to the American expression "Whistle Dixie!" or forget it.

When Papa came home from work that day, his first words were, "What did you prepare for dinner?"

Mama looked him in the eye and gave him a long, low whistle. She had done her thing, meaning, nothing at all.

Mama never cooked for him again. When Papa was home, he was the chef. The only time she prepared dinner was years later when he had the olive oil factory and was out of town making deliveries somewhere. She was almost as good a chef as he was. She didn't have his flair for the artistic arrangement of food, although when it came to taste she was equally masterful.

Chapter Nine
Broken English

The ranch turned out to be a challenge to their relationship in more ways that one. It was not only a social challenge, but a lot of unbelievably hard work. The property included acres of bare land that had never been cultivated. They had a plow, but no horse. That did not stop Orlando. He hitched Filomena to the front of the plow so she could pull while he pushed from the rear and steered their course. Fortunately for Filomena, before too many months she was "with child" so her plowing days were over.

As soon as the ranch was in good working order, Orlando got restless again and moved the family back into town. He started making olive oil, converting an old factory to suit his needs. The oil he produced was of premium quality and was awarded an array of medals and ribbons at the State Fair in Sacramento year after year. At last, he had found an occupation that demanded his skills as a chef and still involved hard physical labor. He settled down to the task of making the best olive oil America had ever tasted. We three daughters were enrolled in school, forcing Filomena to try harder to master the English language.

By then and in spite of herself, Filomena had learned a few words. She could say "Hello" to the friends we brought home and converse with them, even though when she said the word it came out "Allo" The kids understood so it didn't matter. But at school, how she spoke did matter. As we got older, Rina and I were constantly confronted with the fact that our mother spoke broken English.

I remember the first time her inability to pronounce words correctly embarrassed us. We went to school one Monday after our family had gone to a special picnic at a nearby resort the weekend before, the annual According Club Picnic. The highlight of the gathering was a concert by a group of professional accordion players. They were founders of the club and sponsored the huge festivity complete with food, fun, music and dancing. Italians, of course, love all those things. When it comes to music, they are great fans of the accordion. Orlando had had an accordion as a young man and played with a group during his earlier years traveling up and down the coast. Our whole family always had the time of our lives at these picnics.

So Monday morning Rina and I couldn't wait to tell our friends about the wonderful picnic we had been to. "What's the name of the picnic?" they asked.

"The Cording Glube," we said, repeating what we had heard Mama call it.

No one at school knew anything about an event with such a strange name. All day long we tried to tell others about the Cording Glube picnic. Still, no one had a clue what we were talking about. We were surprised, because it was obviously a popular event to draw such a big crowd.

As soon as school was out, we ran home and looked at the admission ticket stubs. Sure enough, they were for the annual Accordion Club Picnic. We were shocked to realize that we had been speaking broken English just like Mama!

From then on, my sisters and I never let her forget each time her tongue failed to enunciate a word correctly. I am sad to have to admit that we laughed at her. Fortunately, she laughed with us. We must have hurt her feelings, but she never let it show.

One of Mama's worse battles with the English language was when she had to telephone the village market to order groceries. In those days, your orders were delivered right to your front door. All you had to do was pick up the telephone and tell the clerk what you wanted.

We traded with a local market whose proprietor was Italian and spoke the language. This made it easier for Mama to order. One morning when she telephoned, the proprietor was gone. The clerk on duty tried his best to understand what she was asking for. He did all right until she asked for a pound of butter. The word "butter" was one she could not pronounce. When she said it, it came out "burr", or worst still, "burrer".

Our telephone was in the hallway and we could hear Mama trying to get the clerk to understand what she wanted. He kept asking her to repeat the word. Finally he said, "I'm sorry, Mrs. Della Maggiora, but I don't know what it is you want."

By then, Mama was exasperated. She resorted to the native language she was comfortable with. "Burro, salame!" she cried, using the Italian word for butter and at the same time calling him a "salame", meaning an Italian meathead.

"Oh, you want a salami!" exclaimed the clerk. "Why didn't you say so?"

Mama hung up the telephone while we rolled on the floor laughing like maniacs. Needless to say, an Italian salami was delivered that morning. We ate it for lunch and relished every bite almost as much as we relished teasing mama about the incident.

Perhaps Mama's funniest verbal misstep happened during a physical emergency when she had to call the doctor. Yes, in those days, doctors made house calls even for minor ailments. It was springtime and all the fruit trees were in bloom. We three sisters were playing out in the yard watching the bees busily working the blossoms. Somehow, my sister Anne managed to get stung on the finger. Immediately, her whole hand started to swell. She ran into the house crying.

When Mama saw her hand, she went right to the telephone and called our family doctor. "Come quickly, Dr. O'Connor!" she told him. "A jackass flew out of the tree and bit Annie on the finger!"

That's one saying we never let her forget.

Mama failed to master the English language, but she knew how to say the right thing at the right time even if the words were mispronounced. It happened years later when I had daughters of my own and we were having dinner at my parents' house. I was fussy about manners and reminded my little girls not to speak when they had food in their mouths. Mama had not been taught any social graces and chewed freely while she was talking.

My daughters were old enough to notice. One of them whispered to me, "Why does Nonna talk with food in her mouth?

Mama heard her. She kept right on chewing as she spoke in perfect broken English. "Because I did not have a mother to teach me important things like that," she said quickly. "But you do. You will never have that bad habit, will you?"

Everyone at the table got the point.

I have spent years trying to learn to speak Italian fluently when I could have learned so easily as a child. Mama was a willing and capable teacher, but I was too busy being an American.

I know one thing. If Mama were here, she would not laugh at me even though I speak very broken Italian.

Chapter Ten
Annual Snipe Hunt

In spite of their unorthodox beginning, Mama and Papa grew to love each other very deeply. I am certain that our close sisterhood had its roots in the relationship our parents had with each other. While Anne began her day with her nose in a book, Rina and I couldn't wait to climb into bed with Mama and Papa as soon as we woke up in the morning and listen to him tell stories.

Papa was at his best as a storyteller. He knew how to embellish the folk tales he had grown up with in Italy and enjoyed telling them as much as we enjoyed listening. He had a rumbling laugh that swept us along with its crescendo. We would snuggle under the covers and beg him to tell just one more, just one more, until it was past time to get ready for school.

One of those stories was about a legendary contest held in Naples, Italy, to choose the Champion Thief of the

World. I revised the story to give it my own personal slant and was thrilled when it was published as a children's book with the title "Orlanda And The Contest Of Thieves". I even put Mama's name, Filomena, in the text. Papa would have liked that book.

I have a tape recording of my father telling about his childhood in Italy and his later adventures in what he always referred to as America. It, too, is interspersed with bursts of laughter. It gives me such pleasure to listen to it. The tape is the poorest quality possible, but listening to it always makes me laugh out loud. He was that kind of a person, my Papa. Mama tamed him considerably, and he needed it, yet that wild, devilish streak colored everything he did.

Once a year Papa threw a shindig at our house, an all-night party with a dance band and food and drinks for everyone. It was held on June 14th, which was Anne's birthday and Flag Day, two good reasons to celebrate. When I say Papa threw a shindig, of course Mama was equally involved. Our double garage had a concrete floor that had to be bleached and waxed for the dance. I don't remember getting in on the cleaning part, but I remember

Rina and I having fun slipping and sliding across the floor to spread the flakes of wax.

Guests started arriving by mid-afternoon, some of them coming from long distances. Our house bulged with makeshift beds, and the whole back yard was a campsite. We loved all the hoopla and especially the dancing. Papa was a born dancer, light on his feet and never missing a beat. He was a tireless host. He danced with everyone, even though the next day he would complain laughingly about what hard work it had been to circle the floor with some of the less graceful women.

Did Papa dance with Mama? I wonder about that now as I write. My memory fails me again. If he did, I don't remember. She wasn't quite five feet tall and the fastest runner on our block, which she proved several times, but music had not been a part of her life in Italy. I guess being an orphan at twelve and having to shoulder the responsibility of four younger siblings didn't leave much room for something as frivolous as dancing.

Papa always provided extracurricular entertainment for our guests in the form of typical Italian pranks. He would invite the town's most derelict bum and set him up with a small barrel of wine anchored high above his head. This was for him alone, to be emptied before nightfall. Papa attached a tube to the spigot on the barrel and put a clamp on it, so all the bum had to do was lay back and guzzle.

Part of the fun was betting if one man on his own could really empty the barrel, which held about two gallons of wine, and still walk home. Oh yes, he had to walk home on his own, too. That was part of the bargain. He was given all he could eat, and the barrel of wine, but he couldn't lose his dignity. He couldn't get so drunk that he was soused. Papa wouldn't have liked that. There was always plenty of wine at our dinner table every night, yet if Papa saw someone drinking more than he could handle, he would deliberately pick up the wine bottles and place them at the other end of the table.

The bum suited Papa's need to create a humorous diversion early in the afternoon. This kept the guests busy checking to see how much was left in the barrel. They also helped keep the bum's plate heaping with food. That man could really eat. By the time the barrel was sucked dry, the band had arrived and it was time to dance. Everyone gathered in the garage to applaud the bum as he ambled down our long driveway on his way home.

Another of Papa's wild schemes was a snipe hunt. This was his favorite prank. He could pull it off only if one of the guests had never been to our house before. Not only did it depend on a newcomer, but the newcomer had to be someone who would not be offended if he were the brunt of a joke.

I remember Papa chuckling softly under his breath as he made the rounds shortly after dark alerting his cronies of his plans. When he had enough volunteers lined up, he would casually ask the designated newcomer if he had ever been snipe hunting. Snipe hunting? What was a snipe? Well, according to Papa it was a cross between a raccoon and a wild pig, but not exactly. Snipes were great fun to hunt, however, and were delicious roasted with plenty of garlic and fresh herbs.

When the unsuspecting visitor went for the bait, Papa would offer to take him snipe hunting that very night. All they needed was a few willing helpers, a sack, and a "bastone", an Italian style bat, alias a two-by-four about three feet long. Several men who had been on one of Papa's previous snipe hunts wasted no time volunteering to go along and introduce the novice to the sport.

No sooner said than done. Papa knew of a place in the mountains just a few miles away that was exactly right for the hunt. They talked about it for a while before he outlined what he thought was the best route to take that night. Everyone drank a toast for good luck. Then Papa and his cronies, armed with sacks and the "bastone", escorted the newcomer to the waiting car.

The rest of the guests waited expectantly for the snipe hunters to return. Rina and I knew that the newcomer himself would not return, at least not for a long time. We had never been on one of Papa's snipe hunts, but we knew the scenario by heart. Once they got to the mountain, they would park the car on a steep grade, set the brake and head out on foot. Everything had to be hush-hush. The snipes had to be caught by surprise or they wouldn't be caught at all.

The group would fan out through the underbrush, being as quiet as possible. At the right moment, Papa would stop and signal for complete silence. This meant he had

97

found a snipe tunnel that met his approval. Indeed it looked very promising. Now it was time to set the trap.

After a little coaxing, everyone agreed to give the newcomer the honor of catching the first snipe. He was shown how to crouch on his knees and hold the sack in front of the opening to the tunnel. Papa and the others would make their way around to the other side and flush the prey out of its hiding place. When the snipe came scurrying out, it would run right into the waiting sack. All the hunter had to do was to tie the end good and tight and carry his prize back to the car. If the snipe gave him too much of a fight, he could whack it on the head with the "bastone".

With the trap set, Papa and his cronies left the eager hunter holding the sack and made their way back down the trail. As soon as they were out of sight, they headed for the parked car as fast as they could. Once inside, they released the brake and coasted downhill. When they reached the bottom of the grade, they slammed the doors shut, started the motor and headed home. Everyone crowded around them as they told and retold the details of the hunt, exaggerating the facts with each telling. It's a wonder the poor snipe hunter didn't hear their bursts of laughter, punctuated with good-natured cheers for his safe return.

Eventually, of course, the newcomer, now properly initiated, would realize that he was the one who had been caught in a trap. Eventually, if he was the good sport he was supposed to be, he would make his way down the mountain and be given a hero's welcome at our house. Not just a hero's welcome, but a hearty invitation to be a volunteer on a snipe hunting expedition the following year.

If my story seems unfairly slanted toward both Papa and Rina, I guess it is because they were very much alike and had an obvious and overwhelming influence on my childhood. Papa was such a character. Like Rina, he was volatile, strong willed and confident, deserving to be called a character. On the other hand, Mama had character. She was the perfect foil for Papa's extroverted personality. Without her, Papa would have been only half a man. And without her influence, I'm afraid I would have had little reason for self-respect.

As much as I enjoyed Papa and his fun-loving ways, when I was ill it was Mama I wanted to care for me. I wasn't sickly like Rina. I was very healthy. Only one disease plagued my childhood. That was poison oak. I suffered from regular bouts with it. I didn't just break out in a rash here and there. Most of my body would become a mass of weeping eruptions that crusted over, leaving me inside a painful, all-encompassing scab. This would last for weeks. I survived by sitting in a recliner chair day and night until the rash dried up and the encrustation could be soaked off.

Mama had had poison oak so she knew what I was going through. Papa had never had it, and in fact it was he who exposed me to it through his clothing. He felt so bad for me, yet I wouldn't let him come near my chair. Mama had to take care of me alone, day and night. She had the gentlest hands imaginable. The slightest touch or movement would cause the awful itching to start again. Somehow she could apply the various salves or compresses without irritating the rash.

In retrospect, I wonder if my bouts with poison oak gave Mama the sole opportunity she had of mothering me. I was such a rebel that it was the only time I allowed her to feel close to me, or me to her. The rest of the time I was too proud and defiant to ask or expect anything from her. I

100

know poison oak doesn't sound like a serious disease, but I had such severe cases of it that it brought me to my knees. It gave me a taste of the hell-fire I had been taught to expect as a sinner.

That sense of being at fault, or more properly of having a sensitive conscience, was Mama's legacy to me. It was her way of trying to teach me to be self-conscious so I would discipline myself and grow up to be a responsible individual. Poor Mama. The role of sinner didn't suit me at all. Neither did the role of saint, for that matter. I tried many roles in my life and the closest I came to feeling at home in any of them was as an independent rebel. That I was!

Oddly enough, the only spanking I got was from Papa, a non-disciplinarian cum laude. One day he asked me to pick up his hat that had fallen to the floor. For some reason, or no reason at all, I refused to do it. Perhaps it was the defiance in my voice that made him pursue the matter. He asked me to pick it up again. By then my feet were set in concrete. I stuck to my "No" and he stuck to his parental right to be able to ask me to do something and expect me to do it. When asking didn't work, he tried demanding. That failed. He tried to reason with me, cajoling me, everything short of bribing me. Rock-head that I was, I wouldn't give in, and Papa finally had to turn me over his knees and paddle my butt.

That spanking hurt him more than it hurt me. I had driven him to do something he was innately against, enforcing discipline. He, of all people, knew about rebellion, rock-headedness and independence. He told me many times about his childhood in Italy, how he had rebelled against the hunger and deprivation forced on him and his family by poverty. His stories were sad, but they were also funny. He would have us all laughing with him as he related one incident after another in his young life.

As a teenager, Papa had a voracious appetite for sausages, but in the Italy of his childhood, you ate meat only on special occasions. And even when they did have it, one or two sausages had to be enough for the entire family. Meat was used to flavor the tomato sauce that was slathered over the nightly fare of pasta or polenta. If the larder was running low on sausage, his stepmother prepared "baccala", salt-dried cod fish, which was placed in the middle of the table where everyone could reach out and dab it with a piece of bread or some polenta. This way you got the flavor of the fish without diminishing it. Used this sparingly, one "baccala" and several strings of sausage could easily last a whole winter.

Meat was so hard to come by that the family supply was kept under lock and key. Papa would look longingly at the chains of fragrant links that hung from the ceiling of the walk-in wire cage that served as a larder in the basement. The cage had a small trap door about a foot off the floor. Should a mouse find its way inside, the cat could dispose of it before it got to the sausage. The cat was kept so well-fed that the suspended meat was relatively safe, but a mouse was a different story.

One time Papa got so hungry for sausage that he couldn't stand it. He caught the cat and kept it in a box without food for a few days. Then he tied a rope around one of its legs and let it through the trap door. The cat didn't waste any time. It made a lunge for the ceiling and pulled down a string of links. Before it could gorge itself on the meat, Papa reeled in the poor animal, retrieved all the sausage except the piece it had in its teeth, and took off with his loot. Later that night, Papa had his fill of the juicy

103

links roasted over an open campfire in the woods behind the house.

The cat trick served Papa well more than once. Sometimes his parents noticed that the sausage supply was getting low quicker than it should. Knowing the kind of child he was, they probably suspected him, but how could he get into the larder without a key? There were only two keys to that lock, and they hung prominently along with the religious medals his parents wore around their necks at all times.

On one occasion, Papa was home alone when he used the cat trick to get his hands on some sausage. Why go out back to his secret campsite to cook it when there were hot coals in the fireplace? So he put the sausages on a skewer and was turning them slowly when he heard the sound of a horse and buggy outside. His father had returned home sooner than expected. What could he do? Any minute the older man would walk in the house and Papa's thievery would be exposed.

While his father was unhitching the buggy, Papa raced around to the back of the barn and started flailing the work horses. They whinnied and reared in their stalls, making a frightful racket. His father heard the commotion and hurried to see what was happening. That gave Papa time to sneak back into the house and retrieve the sausages. To disguise the odor of roasting meat, he threw a handful of eucalyptus leaves on the hot coals and escaped without getting caught.

When Papa told us this story, he would laugh at himself with a mixture of pride and shame. He never forgot his hunger for sausage. It was always one of his favorite meals to prepare for himself and for all of us.

Chapter Eleven

Mama's Italianese

I always felt a kinship with Papa because of his escapades. With such a childhood, surely he could sympathize with my rebellious nature. Mama was saintly by comparison. How could she understand my wild impulses when she had never had any of her own? No doubt this contributed to my distancing myself from her. Considering my attitude, Mama did a masterful job of mothering her "un-motherable", hopelessly American, child.

For all of her life, Mama identified herself as an Italian living in America. Papa thought of himself as an American, albeit of Italian birth. Mama spoke longingly of returning to Italy. Papa found excuses to stay in the USA. It was one of the big regrets of his life that he did not take a trip to Italy with Mama. After her death, we talked him into going back. He had a good time visiting his relatives, but

Italy was no longer his home. This was home, the good old USA, the land of freedom from hunger, the country that had given him a chance to make a life for himself.

Not only was our speech colored by Mama's Italianese, but our clothing was as well. Until we were old enough to be fussy about what we wore, she made all our clothes. Because of her upbringing she was frugal and used whatever material she had on hand. One time when she made a cotton slip cover for the day bed in the hallway she had a couple of yards left over. She decided to use the fabric to make a pair of bloomers for me to wear on my first day at school.

I loved those cotton bloomers and could hardly wait for school to start so I could wear them. I even loved the color. They were a bright orange and black plaid. I guess they satisfied the Italian in me. The fabric was soft, yet it had enough body to hold out my skirt, sort of like a hoop.

Miss Hartley was the kindergarten teacher. I have remembered her all my life because of the part she played in that first day at school. I can see myself, a little Italian kid walking out on the playground wearing those bright plaid bloomers. I was athletic even at that age, so I wasted no time climbing the bars and swinging upside-down. The other kids began laughing. It didn't take long for me to figure out that they were laughing at me, specifically at my bloomers. Their pointed remarks and fingers made it plain.

As soon as the bell rang, I hurried to the classroom, glad for the chance to sit down and pull my skirt over those homemade bloomers. It took Miss Hartley only a few minutes to realize what all the pointing and giggling was about. She immediately called the class to order and introduced herself. Then she invited each of us to stand and give our names. I was close to tears when it was my turn to get up. The next thing I knew, Miss Hartley was standing by my desk. Her face was beaming with pleasure as she put her arms around me, giving me a warm, reassuring hug.

"Did your mother make those lovely bloomers for you, Olga?" she asked, her voice as soft as the cotton fabric Mama had used. "They must be homemade. You can't buy anything as nice as that in a store."

I nodded, unable to speak.

"That's the most beautiful combination of colors I've ever seen!" she continued, hugging me closer. "It's so Italian. Did she get the material in Italy? Do you suppose your mother has enough fabric left over to make something for me?"

The shame and embarrassment I had been feeling rolled off my shoulders like melting snow. Suddenly I was bathing in a mantle of ethnic pride. The look of envy in my classmates' eyes confirmed the discovery I had just made, that Italian and homemade could be beautiful. And while I was not quite ready to openly acknowledge my Italian roots, the mental soil had been prepared for eventual self-recognition.

Chapter Twelve

A Priceless Addition

One bit of Italianese that did not surface in my childhood was the love of hard work. As kids, Rina and I thought work was boring. Mama and Papa worked. Anne worked. We played. So I didn't catch the work ethic until long after Rina, Anne, and I had married and gone our separate ways.

It came almost as a shock to find myself falling in love with an Italian hoe. To me, that particular tool is as Italian as you can get. I was introduced to it by old Dan, the gardener hired by Stella, the woman who in later years became my adopted mom. Dan could do more in a morning with that tool than most men could do ordinarily in a week.

One day I asked Dan if I could use his hoe. I found out why it worked so well and why it was designated as Italian. It is heavy, probably weighing close to seven or eight pounds, with a short handle that is curved where it fits into a slot in the thick, broad blade. If you were strong enough to lift it up, the hoe did the rest. Bend over, lift it up, let it fall. To most people that motion is back breaking. To Italians, "it'sa naturale". I could turn over a huge swath of garden using that hoe, picking it up and letting it slice through the earth as it fell. A slight tug and each chunk of soil turned over just like that.

You don't have to be Italian to use that hoe, but it helps. At one time it was a favorite tool with the migrant workers in our state but unfortunately it was outlawed, condemning it as cruel and unusual punishment. Whoever the officials were that made that decision just weren't Italian. They never got the hang of it, never felt the easy rhythm of its stroke, its almost effortless power. That hefty hoe is back breaking only if you don't know how to use it, if you are not born to it. I discovered that I was born to it, and so was Stella. She was of German descent and well into her senior years, yet she could fuse her body to that tool and produce results almost as amazing as Dan's.

Stella herself was a priceless addition to my life. As my adopted mom, she did for me what I never allowed Mama to do. She found a way for me to learn and

111

appreciate self-respect. It's too bad I wasn't ready for someone like her to come into my life before I had painfully outgrown most of my Italian childhood.

My adoption of Stella was a matter of soul responding to soul. She listened to me talk about my childhood and my feelings toward my mother. She understood what I needed and gently relieved me of the uncomfortable baggage of emotions I had carried with me into adulthood. Little by little, she taught me to be comfortable with myself, past, present and future.

Until Stella started talking to me, I never let myself forget what a willful and headstrong child I had been. And if I did forget temporarily, my family reminded me. To them, I was Olga the rock-head, a reputation I earned the hard way.

One of the revealing stories my family told about me was the time we were riding in the car with Mama and Papa and they bought us each an ice cream cone. I guess I licked mine too hard and the scoop of ice cream fell off. Both Rina and Anne offered to share theirs with me, but I refused to admit I had made a mistake, saying "I've had my part already." It was my way of saving face which was the only self-defense I knew. I had not yet developed the self-confidence to face my shortcomings in order to outgrow them. It was such a minor incident, yet one that both Anne and Rina reminded me of many times.

Little by little, Stella got me to abandon my self defensive attitude. She introduced me to a divine Cause that loved me and was the reason I could love myself. I no longer needed to defend myself. I found my real part in life, a part I had already from the beginning even though, like my Italian connection, I was out of touch with it. I accepted this divine childhood as something I would never tarnish. I could go right on being a child of God. That confidence has become the wind beneath my wings.

A few years ago when I was well beyond the age for such adventures, I went on a river rafting trip down the Colorado in a seven-foot rubber raft without a motor. We capsized and I had to swim through one of the longest and most challenging rapids. It was a test, if ever there was one, and I came through with flying colors. Self-confidence, together with a life jacket, held me above the fear of water. I loved it. Two other passengers panicked and I was able to help them. It is an experience I am proud of. When you are

113

as used to being ashamed, as I was, that feeling of the wind beneath your wings is especially satisfying.

Chapter Thirteen
Seniors' Sneak

When our children were grown and we no longer had family responsibilities, we three sisters started taking trips together once a year. I called them our "seniors' sneak". One of our favorite places was Santa Cruz. We never got over our love for the Boardwalk and the beach. We felt so at home there. And even though Anne still marched to a different drummer, our Italian sisterhood thrived. Each morning, Rina and I got up at dawn and walked miles of the familiar shoreline before Anne was ready to wake up. She was so laid back that we finished eating before she was half way through her meal, and always teased her about how slowly she chewed each bite. Mostly we laughed together, at and with each other. She was never as full of ideas as Rina and I; but she was definitely no longer a dud.

On one of our senior sneaks, we three sisters signed up for a group trip to Spain. Anne shared a room with a good friend of hers, so Rina and I roomed together. Before going to bed every night, Rina got her vitamins ready to take the next morning. She put them in a small dish in plain view so she wouldn't forget them.

We came in late one night after a busy day of sightseeing and hurried to get to bed. Wake up call was at 6 a.m., so Rina was anxious to get to sleep. She changed into nightclothes and took off her jewelry, mainly a gold necklace and matching earrings. The earrings were so small she was afraid she would misplace them. To make sure she didn't, she put them in the same dish with her vitamins.

The next morning we got a late start. Rina was rushing around trying to get ready. Without bothering to put on her eyeglasses first, she took a drink of water, tossed the contents of the dish in her mouth and swallowed.

We went down for breakfast and were chatting away when suddenly Rina felt her ear lobes. No earrings. She looked at me wild-eyed. Then she jumped up, grabbed me by the arm and dragged me back upstairs to our room.

"What's wrong?" I asked anxiously as we took the steps two at a time.

"My earrings!" she cried.

I pictured her earrings going into the same dish as her vitamins the night before. Instantly, I was also wide-eyed. But not for long. I close my eyes when I laugh, and I laughed as hard as I have ever laughed in my life. We both laughed. We sat on the bed and laughed. We hugged each other and laughed. There was no getting around the fact that she was wearing those earrings, all right, but not on her ears.

Eventually we had to go back and join the group. Of course we told them. What else could we do? Poor Anne. She laughed just as much as everyone else did, but I think she was almost ready to renounce us as her sisters.

The story doesn't end there. Rina and I put our heads together and came up with an idea. She would take a strong laxative every night and hope the earrings turned up as nature took its course. That is, if they were not stuck in her intestines somewhere. The pair she swallowed was the kind designed for pierced ears and had sharp posts on the back. The posts came with little locking devices that served

117

as caps, except that in her haste that night when she took them off, Rina had not capped them.

For three days, Rina spent her mornings in the bathroom while the rest of us had breakfast. But it worked. On the third day, she came downstairs beaming. Both earrings were eliminated and retrieved.

When we got back home, Rina took the earrings to a good jeweler who cleaned and polished the gold as good as new. I don't think Rina told him about swallowing them. It's a shame she didn't. Just think of the laughs he would have gotten relating that experience to his customers.

One Christmas Rina dressed up as Santa Claus for our family gathering, which was always a huge affair as much for the adults as for the kids. After she handed gifts to the little ones and ho-ho-hoed her way out the front door, she decided to treat the neighbors to a surprise visit from Santa. I drove her up and down the street as she knocked on doors spreading good cheer. Before long we got bored and wondered why we should limit ourselves to the neighborhood. Why not go for broke? So we drove down town and found a pub in full swing and decided to give the patrons a real holiday feeling. And I do mean feeling.

She disguised her voice so the patrons presumed she was man. When Santa asked a few of the women for a dance they loved it. Rina was an excellent dancer and even though she was not very tall she took them for a good spin. Being Rina, she couldn't resist giving each one a little extra "holiday feeling" they didn't expect and they loved it all the more. But when "Santa" started making passes at the men, she had the whole pub in an uproar. They didn't want him/her to leave and we barely got out of there without a riot.

Yes, life is good, and being Italian is as good as it gets.

Which brings this story of my childhood full circle. It all tallies at last except for one thing. I hope Mama is listening.

"You were right, Mama. I am Italian as well as American, even though it took me more than three-quarters of a century to realize it."

The End

Author's Note

Anne passed away before I finished writing this story so she never had the chance to read it. Fortunately, Rina did get to read it, though she too has now gone. Her precious note of approval follows: *"You couldn't have done a better job. Reading it, I relived my life again. Thanks again for remembering, and for loving me. With tears streaming down my face, I again say thank you. I am very proud of you as my little sister."*

Rina, my all

About the author

You are invited to visit the author's web site, www.olgacossi.com for an introduction to her books for young readers and her stories behind the stories. You can also listen to her broadcasts as part of First Person Singular on KUSP, Santa Cruz, where she tells a story in ninety seconds. Search for her name at www.blogs.kusp.org/firstperson.

Rafting the Colorado

Olga now

Acknowledgments
To Hedi, Joanna and Mathilde, not sisters, but talented
assisters whose help make this book possible.

My "adopted Mom", Stella

Other nonfiction memoirs published by Solstice Publishing:

SMOOTH TRAVELING FOR SENIORS

Jack Adler

Concerned over health while traveling? Interested in discounts and bargains for seniors? Want to know how to make hassle-free reservations online?
How to insure personal and currency security while on the road? These, and many related subjects, are comprehensively covered in this book.

It's filled with practical information and pointers on what senior travelers should know and do – or not do – in various situations.

Among the many other subjects are how to research travel and plan itineraries, using foreign government tourist offices and state/city tourism offices in the U.S., dealing with new phone technology and applications, dining sense, traveling in groups or independently, shopping and bargaining, passports/documents, avoiding scams, etc.

A vast roster of key topics comprising the overall travel world of today that pertain to seniors are covered in easy-to-use chapters that will make every travel outing, domestic or international, a more enriching and valuable experience.

Many little-known but useful tips provide travel-enhancing information on every mode of travel and to every part of the world.

The plethora of Internet links provided is worth the cover-price alone!

Jack Adler is a veteran travel writer, with over 25 years of covering the travel field for both consumer and trade publications. His credits include several travel books published: *Consumer's Guide To Travel, Exploring Historic California, Southern India, Make Steady Money As A Travel Writer – Without Traveling, There's A Bullet Hole In Your Window (memoir),* and *Travel Safety* (co-authored). *Splendid Seniors: Great Lives, Great Deeds,* while non-travel, also is about seniors.

DOWN HOME
Memories of a small brained Okie

Bud Crawford

An amusing slice of Americana, written in an inimitable style. Everyone has great plans and ideas when they're growing up. Some work and some don't. For Stanley and me, our motto could have been "It seemed like a great idea at the time". Unfortunately, judging by the outcome of most of our ideas, our theme song should have been the music from the Three Stooges. We never really learned from our mistakes. We just figured we'd done it wrong the first time and needed to try it again to get it right.

If you've ever buried your best friend while he was alive; if you've ever found yourself hanging from a tree limb knowing the only way you were going to get down was to fall; if you've ever had your hand stuck in a hole in a riverbank trying to catch a catfish, then these stories should bring back fond memories.
And if you haven't, then welcome to the world of a couple of Okie kids in the 1960s.

In the days when kids could still roam the woods on escapades. When they slept outdoors without fear. Those days before 'health and safety' killed imagination and became a watchword for dull and boring.

Be warned, if you're an animal lover, some creatures were harmed in the making of this life. Nature in the raw – tooth and claw – and a few bites and stings along the way…

HOOKED

Jim Baugh

Hooked is based on the true-life story of Virginia outdoor television producer Jim Baugh. Jim Baugh Outdoors TV is one of Americas most diverse and entertaining outdoor programs and has been in syndication since 1989.

Hooked is a hilarious look behind the scene stories of filming a southern outdoor TV show. From the Chesapeake Bay to Key West these on location excursions will make your sides hurt with laughter. A cast of sea faring characters full of color and humor. From the docks in Gloucester Virginia to the Atlantic Ocean and a boat load of jolly swashbuckling Pirates. The stories and characters are timeless and span a period of over forty years.

In contrast, *Hooked* also explores the solemn drama of dealing with divorce, death, and mental illness.

The story also delves into the totally crazy insane world of mid-life on-line computer dating. This is a hilarious look at dating in the computer world after 25 years of solid marriage. These dating stories are contemporary, racy, scary, cheerful, timeless, and based on true events. Anyone who is old enough to date will soon relate to *Hooked* as the comical reference for dating in the new millennium.

This adult romantic comedy story also relates to the power and testament of faith.

50 Years of an exciting action packed extremely charismatic colorfull life and career, packed into 28 chapters. It's a fast ride, for sure.

Jim Baugh has been producing National and Regional television shows for 25 years. Programs include: Jim Baugh Outdoors TV (220 episodes), Ski East, Classic Fishing. Fishing Virginia and, RV Times. Jim Baugh has written over 300 columns for numerous magazines during the last 20 years including: *Motor boating Magazine, Fishing Smart, The Chesapeake Angler, The Sportsman Magazine* and *Travel Virginia Magazine.*

THE TALE OF WISDOM AND DELIGHT

Mari LaFore

This is the true and inspirational story of two cats and reincarnation. It's also about love, devotion and loss. And belief.

Mari LaFore combines her heart-knowledge of her pet's reincarnation with documentation and expert opinion to create a beautiful and credible testimony. As an author, I enjoyed having LaFore's loving words about her cats dance up and down my spine. Kudos on a warm and soul-satisfying story! – Pegi Deitz Shea

"A wonderful story of love and hope." - Megan Zuba, Case Manager, St. Joseph Center, Los Angeles, CA.

"If you love animals, you'll adore this book!" – Helen Ross, reviewer

Made in the USA
Charleston, SC
25 June 2012